The BIGGEST BULLY in Brookdale

Carol Gorman

Illustrated by Rudy Nappi

Publishing House
St. Louis

To my friend
Joan Lowery Nixon
with gratitude and affection

Published by Concordia Publishing House
3558 S. Jefferson Avenue, St. Louis, MO 63118-3968
Manufactured in the United States of America

Library of Congress Cataloging in Publication Data.

Gorman, Carol
The biggest bully in Brookdale by Carol Gorman; illustrated by Rudy Nappi.
(The Tree House Kids)
Summary: When Tess and Ben fail in their attempts to get even with school bully Brad, Mrs. Pilkington suggests praying for him.
ISBN 0-570-04713-7
[1. Bullies—Fiction. 2. Schools—Fiction. 3. Christian life—Fiction.] I. Nappi, Rudy, ill. II. Title. III. Series: Gorman, Carol. Tree House Kids.

PZ7.G6693Bi 1992
[Fic]—dc20
91-40590
CIP

---

1 2 3 4 5 6 7 8 9 10 01 00 99 98 97 96 95 94 93 92

Series

The Biggest Bully in Brookdale
It's Not Fair

Contents

The Bully

"Did you hear about the new kid?" Ben asked.

"What new kid?" Tess asked.

"He moved here this summer," Ben said. "I heard he's tough."

"Really?" Tess said.

"And mean," Ben said.

Ben Brophy and Tess Munro were walking to school on the first day of third grade. Tess lived next door and was Ben's best friend. Ever since kindergarten, they had walked to school together almost every day.

Ben wore a new pair of jeans and a red shirt. Tess's blond hair was pulled back and tied with a bright yellow ribbon. Both Ben and Tess carried backpacks over their shoulders. The packs were stuffed full with back-to-school supplies.

"So what's this kid's name?" Tess asked.

"Brad," Ben said. "Brad Garth. He's a fourth grader."

"Oh," Tess said.

"And I hear he's big," Ben said.

"Does he beat up on girls?" Tess asked.

"He beats up on everybody!" Ben said. "It's his hobby."

Tess made a face. "That's a dumb hobby. I like climbing trees and playing badminton."

"Yeah, me too," said Ben.

Ben and Tess walked along the sidewalk. The sun was shining, and the air smelled cool and fresh.

"I hope I don't ever see that guy," Ben said.

"If he's in fourth grade, you'll have to see him sometime," Tess pointed out. "The fourth-grade room is right next to ours."

"Yeah," Ben said.

"And you'll see him on the playground," Tess said.

"I guess so," Ben said.

"And he'll be in the boys' bathroom," Tess said.

"This is going to be a horrible year," Ben said.

"No, it's not," Tess said. "Third grade will be fun."

"Not if Brad Garth beats up on all the kids," Ben said. "That won't be fun."

"The teachers won't let him," Tess said. "And Mr. Evans is a strict principal. He won't let Brad Garth get away with picking on kids."

"I hope you're right," Ben said.

"This year will be fun," Tess said. "Third graders get to do more things than second graders."

"Like what?" Ben asked.

"Remember last year when Ms. Conley's class got to go to the science museum?" Tess asked.

"Yeah," Ben said. "That sounded awesome."

"I heard the kids saw the skeleton of a dinosaur!" Tess said. "I can't wait to see that!"

"Ms. Conley is hard," Ben said.

"But nice," Tess said.

"I hope so," Ben said.

"Quit worrying," Tess said.

"Who's worrying?" Ben said.

But Ben was worried. He was a little nervous about starting a new school year with a hard teacher, even though the kids all thought she was nice. But most of all, Ben was scared about the new kid, Brad Garth. But he didn't want Tess to know he was scared. She didn't seem frightened at all!

Tess stopped when they got to the corner. "Want to take the shortcut? It's not muddy or anything."

The shortcut went through a woodsy part of the neighborhood next to the park.

Ben shrugged. "Sure."

Ben and Tess headed into the woods.

It was quiet among the trees, away from people's voices and the *swish, swish* of the cars on the street.

Some of the trees were just beginning to turn red and orange. Their leaves fluttered gently in the soft morning breeze.

"I wish we didn't have to go back to school," Ben said.

"I'm glad," Tess said. "Summer's great,

but sometimes it gets kind of boring at home."

"Boring?" said Ben. He couldn't believe what he was hearing. "In the summer, you can go swimming, fishing, camping, picnicking, biking, roller-skating, tree climbing—"

"Yeah, but even that gets boring sometimes," Tess said. "Anyway, I'm glad to get back to school and see all the kids again."

"You saw most of them at the swimming pool every day," Ben said.

"Yeah," Tess said. "But, still . . ."

Just then, they heard a yell.

"What was that?" Tess asked.

They heard another yell, even louder this time.

"Sounds like someone's in trouble," Ben said.

"Come on!" Tess said.

Ben and Tess hurried along the path, which ran up a slope between the trees.

At the top of the slope, they stopped in their tracks.

Not far away from them were two kids, one big and one little. The big kid grabbed the little kid's shirt just under his chin. He made a fist with his other hand and held it up in front of the little kid.

"Give it to me!" the big kid growled.

"It's my dad's!" the little kid cried. He wore big glasses that slid down his nose. His eyes were filled with fear.

"I said give it to me!" the big kid yelled into the little kid's face.

"Okay, okay," the little kid said, his voice trembling. "But my dad's going to kill me."

The big kid laughed. "Good for your dad. Then I won't have to do it."

The little kid reached into his book bag and pulled out a wallet. He handed it over to the big kid.

The big kid grabbed it from the boy, then shoved him to the ground.

"And if you tell anyone, midget, I'll whip you good," the big kid said.

Then the big kid turned and walked away on the path toward school.

The Tree House

The little kid was still sprawled on the ground. Ben and Tess ran to him.

"Are you okay?" Ben asked him.

"Well," the little kid said, pushing his glasses up on his nose, "let's say I've been better."

Ben and Tess pulled the kid to his feet.

"What's your name?" Tess asked.

"Roger," the kid said. "Roger Quinn."

"I'm Ben Brophy. That's Tess Munro. And I think we've just met Brad Garth."

Roger's eyes got big. "Brad Garth? I've heard of him! I hear he eats little kids for breakfast."

"Oh, brother," Tess said, rolling her eyes. "Nobody does that!"

"Well, he sure is mean!" Roger said.

"How am I going to tell my dad I lost all of my lunch money for the week?"

"Tell your dad the truth," Ben said. "Tell him a big bully came and took it from you."

"Yeah," Roger said. "The biggest bully in Brookdale."

"Right," Ben said.

"I'll try it," Roger said. "I hope Dad understands."

Roger picked up his book bag and slung it over his shoulder.

"What grade are you in?" Tess asked.

"Second," Roger said.

"You seem pretty smart for a second grader," Tess said.

"I like to read," Roger said. "Everything I know comes from books. What grade are you two in?"

"Third," Ben said.

"And the Beast?" asked Roger.

"You mean Brad Garth?" Ben asked.

"Yeah," said Roger. "Brad the Beast. What grade is he in? Fifth? Sixth?"

"No, he's in fourth," said Ben.

"He sure is big for a fourth grader," Roger said.

"He sure is," Ben said.

"We'd better get going," Tess said. "We don't want to be late for school."

The three kids headed toward Mark Twain Elementary. Even from a block away, they could see lots of kids inside the metal fence on the playground, swarming around the building.

Just then the bell rang.

"That's the first bell," Tess said. "Let's run."

Ben, Tess, and Roger ran the rest of the way to school. Ms. Conley and the other teachers stood by the front door.

"Please line up according to your grade," Ms. Conley called out.

"First grade here!" yelled a tall, dark-haired woman, who must have been a new teacher this year.

"Second grade over here!" called out Mrs. Trent, holding up her hand.

"I wish we could have Mrs. Trent again," Ben said. "She was so nice."

"You'll have her for second grade," Tess said to Roger. "Go line up."

Roger gave Tess a salute and walked over to the second-grade line.

Ben and Tess got in Ms. Conley's line. Ben looked around.

"Where's Brad Garth? Do you see him?" he whispered to Tess.

"No," she said, looking back over her shoulder. "Oh, there he is!" She pointed to the far corner of the school building.

Ben looked where Tess pointed, and there was Brad. He was leaning up against the school building, his arms folded over his chest. He was watching the kids line up, but he didn't move to follow his teacher's instructions.

The second bell rang, and the kids filed into the school.

"Your names are posted on your lockers," Ms. Conley said. "Put your sweaters or jackets in your lockers and come on into the classroom."

Ben found his locker on the very end of the third-grade section of lockers. There was a little space on the wall, and then the lockers for the fourth graders began.

Ben opened his locker, took everything out of his book bag, and hung the bag inside. He closed the locker door.

When Ben looked up, he caught his breath.

There, on the end of the fourth-grade lockers, was the name *Brad* in big, black letters. Brad Garth's locker was practically right next to Ben's!

Ben's heart started to thump hard in his chest. He didn't see Brad anywhere, but he hurried into his classroom, just in case.

The school day went fast. There was so much to do to get set up in their desks with all of their supplies. Ben's desk was too short, so the custodian came and adjusted it to fit him.

Tess had been right. Ms. Conley was very nice, but she made it clear that she expected her students to work hard.

Ben didn't see Brad Garth for the rest of the school day. Brad didn't even come to his locker after school was dismissed in the afternoon.

Ben and Tess found Roger Quinn waiting for them on the sidewalk a half-block from school.

"Want to walk home with us?" Tess asked.

"Yeah," he said. "But let's not go through the woods."

"Good idea," Ben said.

"You mean," Tess said, "for the rest of the year we can't walk through the woods because Brad Garth might be there?"

"Do you want to meet up with Brad the Beast?" Roger asked her.

"No," Tess said. "But that isn't fair! We should be able to walk anywhere we want to if our parents say it's okay."

"I know," Ben said.

Roger cleared his throat. "Well," he said, squinting through his big glasses, "if you ever had a close-up look at Brad Garth's fist, you wouldn't want to see it again either."

Tess frowned. "Well, what are we going to do?" she said.

"Let's stick together," Ben said.

"Good idea," said Roger. "He'd never try and beat up all three of us!"

Just then, the kids heard footsteps slapping the sidewalk behind them. They turned just in time to see Brad Garth running toward them, his arms folded up close to his chest as if he were carrying a football.

"Outta my way!" he yelled. "Or I'll knock

you out of the stadium! Nobody can tackle Brad Garth!"

Ben, Tess, and Roger scampered off of the sidewalk, but that didn't help at all.

Brad, yelling at the top of his voice, swerved off the sidewalk and bumped into Tess, knocking her to the ground.

Then his shoulder crashed into Ben's arm. Ben staggered but didn't fall down.

"We meet again, midget," Brad hollered at Roger. With a flick of his fingers, he grabbed Roger's glasses from his face and flung them into the grass.

"Good-bye, you twerps!" Brad yelled. "Stupid, little twerps!"

He ran off down the sidewalk.

"That bully!" Tess cried, leaping to her feet. "I hate that kid!"

"Did your glasses break?" Ben asked Roger, rubbing his aching arm.

"No," Roger said, looking at his glasses carefully. "He threw them into the grass. They're okay." He put them back on his face.

"We have to do something about that guy!" Tess said.

"Yeah, but what?" Ben said.

"I don't know," Tess said. "Something."

The kids started off toward home.

"Hey," Roger said, "will you guys walk the rest of the way home with me?" He still looked a little scared.

"Sure," Tess said. "Where do you live?"

"On Robin Hood Road," Roger said. "It's not far."

Roger led Ben and Tess over several streets and into an unfamiliar neighborhood.

"Let's go through Mrs. Pilkington's back yard," Roger said. "I live right next door."

Ben and Tess followed Roger into a large yard behind a big white house.

"Wow! A tree house!" Ben said, looking up into a large oak tree next to the garage.

Tess looked where Ben was staring. She gasped.

"It's beautiful!" she said.

The tree house, made of dark-stained boards, rested in the branches of the oak, which towered over the garage.

"That's Mrs. Pilkington's tree house," Roger said. "She lets me climb up there." He looked at Ben and then Tess. "Want to see it?"

"Sure!" the kids cried out together.

"Follow me," Roger said.

"Where's the ladder?" Tess asked, looking around the tree. "How do you get up there?"

"Watch," Roger said.

He moved to the side of the garage. A chain-link fence, which surrounded most of Mrs. Pilkington's yard, ended right next to the garage.

Roger poked a toe through the metal mesh in the fence and climbed to the top of the fence. Then he pulled himself onto the garage roof.

"See?" he said. "It's easy! From here, you can climb right into the tree house."

Ben and Tess giggled and followed Roger up to the top of the garage. Roger stepped up into the tree house, then offered his hand to Ben and Tess.

The three kids stood silently for a moment and looked out over the neighborhood.

"You can see everything from up here!" Tess whispered.

"There's my house," Roger said, pointing to the small, gray house next door.

"This is great!" Ben said.

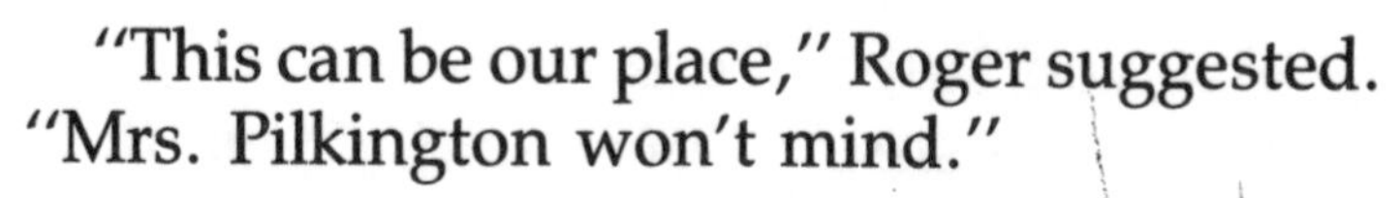

"This can be our place," Roger suggested. "Mrs. Pilkington won't mind."

"Are you sure?" Tess said.

"Sure, I'm sure!" Roger said. "Mrs. P. is a really nice lady."

"We can have a club!" Tess said. "And we'll figure out what to do about Brad Garth."

"Great idea!" Roger said. "But we need a name. Every club has to have a name."

"That's easy," Ben said.

Tess and Roger looked at Ben, waiting for him to say the name.

Ben put one arm around Tess's shoulder. He put the other arm around Roger's shoulder.

"We're The Tree House Kids!" he said.

"I like it!" Tess said.

"Me too!" Roger said.

The three kids grinned at each other and then looked out over the yards and housetops.

"That's it," Tess said. "We'll stick together and get Brad Garth to stop bullying every kid at school!"

"Right!" Roger said.

"Nothing can stop The Tree House Kids!" Ben said.

The Plan

"Roger?" the woman's voice said from below. "Is that you?"

The kids had been sitting on the floor of the tree house plotting a way to get Brad Garth to leave them alone. Roger, hearing the voice, scrambled to his feet and peered over the wooden-plank wall that came up to his shoulders.

"Hi, Mrs. Pilkington," he called out. "Want to come up?"

"Sure," she said.

Ben and Tess stood up and looked over the wall. They saw a slender, gray-haired woman dressed in jeans and a red blouse climbing up the fence.

"Isn't she kind of old to be climbing up here?" Tess whispered to Roger.

"Mrs. P.'s used to that kind of stuff," he said. "She's a skydiver."

Tess's eyes got big. "She jumps out of airplanes?" she said.

"You're kidding!" Ben said. "She's as old as my grandmother!"

Roger grinned. "Mrs. P.'s really awesome," he said.

In a moment, Mrs. Pilkington stepped into the tree house from the garage.

"Hello, Roger," she said. "You brought some friends along, I see."

"Yeah," Roger said. "This is Ben Brophy and Tess Munro."

"Hi, Ben," she said. "Hi, Tess."

The two kids said hi.

"You like the tree house?" Mrs. Pilkington asked.

"Yeah!" Ben said.

"It's great up here," Tess said.

"Yes, it is," Mrs. Pilkington said. She nodded at Roger. "Roger spent half of the summer up here reading." She smiled. "My husband built this house for our son about 20 years ago. He's grown-up now and has a family of his own. So I'm glad a new set of kids can enjoy the house."

"We're going to have a club," Roger said. "The Tree House Kids."

"Terrific!" said Mrs. Pilkington.

"We're banding together to figure out how to get a big kid at school to stop beating up other kids," Tess said.

"Especially us," Roger said.

"Hmmm," said Mrs. Pilkington. "That does sound like a problem."

"Boy, it sure is!" Tess said.

"He's big!" Ben said.

"He's mean!" Tess said.

"He eats little kids for dessert!" Roger said.

"Well, not exactly," Tess said, rolling her eyes. "But something has to be done about him, that's for sure!"

The three kids and Mrs. Pilkington sat on the tree-house floor.

"What are you thinking of doing about this kid?" asked Mrs. Pilkington.

"Well," Tess said hopefully, "I thought maybe we could get Susie Halstead's big brother in sixth grade to beat him up for us."

"Wow," said Mrs. Pilkington, "that sounds kind of dangerous."

Roger frowned behind his big glasses.

"This is a dangerous situation, Mrs. P.," he said. "There are lives at stake here."

Mrs. Pilkington nodded thoughtfully.

"You know," she said, "whenever you have a problem, you can ask God to help you."

"Yeah," Roger said, "but we need somebody to beat up Brad Garth. I don't think God does stuff like that."

"No, I don't think so," said Mrs. Pilkington with a little smile. "But maybe there's another way to handle him. God would know what to do."

"You mean, without beating him up?" Tess asked doubtfully.

"Right," Mrs. Pilkington said.

"But Brad's tough," Roger said. "And probably not very smart. I bet a good sock in the nose is all he'd understand."

"Well," said Mrs. Pilkington. "I think you're likely to get more trouble than you have now. Violence never solves anything."

"Maybe we need a bodyguard!" said Tess. "Just the threat of a sock in the nose might be enough. If Brad thinks somebody might beat him up if he bothers us, he'd probably leave us alone!"

"That's a great idea!" Ben said. "Susie Halstead's brother could protect us! He

could tell Brad he'd better leave us alone! You're right, Mrs. Pilkington. Maybe we won't need to punch him out, after all."

"Well," Mrs. Pilkington said doubtfully, "I think you three could use better help than a big sixth grader."

"You mean God?" Ben asked.

"Yes," said Mrs. Pilkington. "Why don't you ask Him?"

Ben shrugged. "Okay," he said.

"Yeah," Roger said. "When I say my prayers tonight, I'll ask God for help."

"Me too," Tess said.

"Good," said Mrs. Pilkington. "God wants to help people with their problems, you know."

"Yeah, that's what my Sunday school teacher says," Ben added.

"And you don't have to wait until bedtime prayers to talk to God," Mrs. Pilkington said. "You can talk to Him anytime. He's always there, listening."

"Okay," Tess said. "I think you're right, Mrs. P. I bet God wouldn't want us to get beaten up by a maniac like Brad Garth."

Mrs. Pilkington stood up and smiled. "I'm sure He wouldn't either, Tess. Well,

I've got to go to my aerobics class now. I'll be anxious to hear how everything works out."

"Thanks, Mrs. P.," said Roger. "And thanks for the use of your clubhouse."

"Any time," said Mrs. Pilkington. "You're all welcome here."

The kids waved good-bye to Mrs. Pilkington, who stepped over to the garage roof and disappeared down the side.

"Maybe Mrs. P.'s right," Roger said. "Let's ask God to help Susie Halstead's brother look really big and mean so we won't have to use violence."

"Good idea," Tess said.

Ben nodded. "God wouldn't want us to have Brad Garth beaten up anyway," he said.

"No," Tess said. "God isn't like that."

"So," Ben said, "let's pray for Susie Halstead's brother to look so scary, Brad Garth will never beat up another person."

"Right!" said Tess and Roger.

They grinned at each other. Maybe Brad Garth could be scared into leaving them alone!

David Halstead: Bodyguard

"It's all set," Ben said to Tess over the phone the next morning. "Susie Halstead's brother is going to meet us at the edge of the woods."

"Good!" Tess said. "I'll call Roger and tell him to be there."

"Great," Ben said.

"Did you pray last night?" Tess asked

"Yup," Ben said. "I asked God to make Susie Halstead's brother—hey, what's her brother's name anyway?"

"I think it's David," Tess said.

"Oh," Ben said. "Well, I asked God to make David really scary."

"Me too," Tess said. "Let's hope this works. See you out front in five minutes."

"Right," Ben said. He hung up.

Ben's little brother was watching him.

"Who was that?" Grady asked. He was only four and not in school yet.

"That was Tess," Ben said.

"Why do you want someone to be scary?" Grady asked. "Is it Halloween?"

"No," Ben said. "This big kid is beating up on other kids, and we want to scare him so he'll stop."

"Ohhhhhh," Grady said. He frowned and looked worried. "I don't want to meet him."

"Who?" Ben said.

"I don't want to meet a scary person," Grady said. "And I don't want to meet a guy who beats up other kids."

"Yeah," Ben said. "I know what you mean."

Ben said good-bye to his mother, who kissed him and handed him his lunch sack. At least Brad Garth wouldn't be likely to steal his lunch. He wanted lunch *money*.

Ben met Tess on the sidewalk. They walked quickly to the edge of the woods, where they found Roger and David Halstead waiting.

David was even bigger than he had been at the end of the school year last spring. Ben looked at his muscles and felt happy. Brad Garth would never mess with them if a big guy like David was protecting them!

"Where is this punk?" David asked, slamming his fist into his other hand. He looked as if he would like to meet Brad Garth.

"We saw him in the woods yesterday," Tess said.

"He took my lunch money," Roger said. He turned to Ben. "By the way, my dad didn't kill me. In fact, he said he'd talk to the principal if I wanted him to."

"I think this plan with David should work," Ben said.

"Just let me at him," David said. He gritted his teeth and looked really scary. Ben, Tess, and Roger grinned at one another.

The four kids followed the path into the woods.

"Yesterday it was like he was waiting for me," Roger said. "He was leaning against a tree at the top of the slope."

"He wanted to steal someone's lunch

money," Tess said. "He was probably waiting for anyone to come along."

"Anyone smaller than he is," Roger added.

The kids made their way through the woods and up the slope.

"There!" Roger whispered. "There he is again!"

Brad Garth was sitting on a tree stump not far from where he'd stolen Roger's wallet yesterday.

"Stand back," David Halstead said. He clenched his hands into fists and marched over to Brad Garth.

Ben, Tess, and Roger moved over to a clump of bushes and peeked out from behind them to watch what was going on.

David reached down and hauled a surprised Brad Garth to his feet.

"Hey," Brad said angrily.

"Listen to me, Brat," David said.

"The name's Brad," Brad said in a little voice.

"Oh, sorry, *Brat*," David said. "Listen, I hear you've been picking on some friends of mine." He gave Brad a shake. "If I ever

hear you've messed with them again, you can look forward to a punch in the nose." He shoved his face close to Brad's. "I like punching noses. Get it?"

Brad nodded.

"Good," David said. He dropped Brad back onto the tree stump. "Watch yourself, Brat."

David turned and walked back to the kids.

"Oh, that was great!" Ben said, slapping David on the back.

"Yeah, thanks," Tess said.

"That should do it," said Roger.

The kids looked over at Brad Garth. He was still sitting on the tree stump. He was watching them, and he looked very angry.

Ben, Tess, and Roger met on the sidewalk after school. They were all in good moods.

"Let's take the shortcut home!" Ben said. "It should be safe now."

"Yeah," Tess said. "Isn't it great to have our freedom back?"

They tromped along the sidewalk and turned into the woods. They walked into its depths, where it was darkest. Only a little of the afternoon sunlight filtered down to the ground.

Tess suddenly grabbed Ben and Roger. "Look!" she whispered. "It's Brad Garth!"

Sure enough, Brad was walking along the path toward them. He looked angry.

"So you got the big guy to fight for you," he said.

"You'd better not bug us!" Tess said. "David Halstead will make you sorry!"

"Oh, yeah?" Brad said. He walked over to Tess and shoved her to the ground.

"Ow!" Tess cried. Her hand had landed on a prickly plant.

"Stop that!" Ben yelled. "You leave Tess alone!" He wanted to run and punch Brad, but Brad was so much bigger than he was. Ben knew it would be useless.

"What are you going to do about it?" said Brad. "I don't see your big friend around here to protect you."

"I'll tell him!" Ben said.

"He can't protect you when he isn't here," Brad said, sneering. "And if David beats me up, I'll just beat you up even worse!"

Ben swallowed hard. He knew Brad meant it.

Brad grinned wickedly, then turned and disappeared down the path.

Ben, Tess, and Roger looked at one another with worried faces.

"Well," Roger said, glancing back and forth from Ben to Tess, "what do we do *now?*"

It's a Ghost!

Ben, Tess, and Roger sat on the tree-house floor.

"I just can't understand it!" Tess asked. "I was sure David Halstead would scare Brad into leaving us alone!"

"Well, it didn't work," Ben said. "So we'd better come up with another plan."

"How else can we scare him?" Tess asked.

"Well, big kids don't seem to do the job," Ben said. "David is as big as they come!"

"Heck, I don't think he's scared of *humans!*" Roger said.

Ben sat up straight, and his eyes got big. "How about if we scare him with something that *isn't* human?" he said.

"What do you mean?" Tess asked.

"What about a ghost?" Ben said.

"There's no such thing as ghosts," Roger said.

"But maybe we could convince Brad that there *are* ghosts!" Ben said, grinning.

"Hey, yeah," Roger said, his eyes lighting up. "Like in the movie *A Christmas Carol.* We could have the Ghost of Brad's Future come and tell him how lonely he's going to be if he's mean to everybody!"

"That would never work," Tess said, shaking her head. "He'd know it was us."

"Not if it's over the phone," Ben said. "We could disguise our voices."

Tess made a face. "Who ever heard of a ghost that makes telephone calls?"

"So this is a new kind of ghost that uses modern technology!" Roger said.

"Technology?" Ben said. "Roger, are you sure you're only in second grade?"

"Maybe it would work," Tess said.

"What do we have to lose?" Roger asked.

"Nothing!" Tess and Ben said together.

"Let's do it right now," Roger said. "We can use the telephone in my house." He looked back and forth between Tess and Ben. "Who's going to be the ghost?"

The three kids practiced scary voices and decided Ben's was the most frightening.

They climbed down from the tree and trooped into Roger's house.

"Where's your mom?" Tess asked Roger. Roger had unlocked the door with the key that dangled from a string around his neck.

"She's getting a perm," Roger said. "She'll be home soon."

"Where's the phone?" Ben said.

"Use the one in the kitchen," Roger said.

"I have a great idea!" Ben said. "Do you have a chain to lock up your bike?"

"Sure," Roger said, puzzled. "Why?"

"Get it," Ben said. "You can rattle it in the background."

"Yeah!" Tess said. "Ghosts are supposed to rattle chains."

"The perfect authentic detail!" Roger said. He opened a side door in the kitchen and disappeared into the garage. When he returned a moment later, he held his bicycle chain.

Ben looked up Brad Garth's number in the school phone book. After speaking a few practice sentences in his ghost voice to warm up, he dialed the number.

"Hello?" Brad answered.

"Hello-ooooooo!" Ben said in his spookiest voice.

"Who's this?" Brad said. He sounded gruff and mean.

"This is Your Futur-rrrrrre, Brad Garth!" Ben said.

"My what?" Now Brad sounded angry.

"Your Futur-rrrrrre!" Ben said. "Brad Garth, you're a mean and nasty kiiiiiiiiid!" Ben motioned to Roger to rattle his chain. Roger held the chain up close to the phone and clinked it together.

"Who is this?" Brad said, now sounding not quite so sure of himself.

"I already to-ooooooold you!" Ben wailed.

"What do you want?" Brad said.

Ben wasn't sure, but Brad seemed a little scared. Maybe this was going to work!

"If you keep acting mean, you're going to be sor-rrrrrrrrry!" Ben said. "You'll be lonely and forgotten and everybody will haaaaaaaaaaate you!"

That seemed to put Brad in a bad mood. "Who ever heard of a ghost that uses the telephone?" He sounded crabby.

"I'm a new kind of ghost that uses modern . . ."

Ben couldn't remember Roger's word. "Moder-rrrrrn stuff."

"Technology," Roger whispered.

"Yeah, technology," Ben wailed.

"Hey," Brad said angrily, "Now I know who you are! You're the kids who got a bodyguard to defend you! I can hear the midget with the glasses in the background!"

"Nooooooooo!" Ben wailed. He could feel his heart beating hard. "You're wroooooooooong!"

"Boy, wait till I get my hands on you guys tomorrow!" Brad said. "Just wait!"

An Experiment

"So what do we do now?" Roger asked. "Anybody have an idea?"

The kids had walked out Roger's backdoor and were sitting on the porch steps.

"Brad's going to be looking for us tomorrow for sure," Ben said. "He really sounded mad!"

"I don't want Brad to beat us up," Tess said, her eyes wide with fear. "He hates us now for getting a sixth-grade bodyguard and for trying to scare him on the phone."

"Yeah," Roger said. "He was a bully before all of that happened. Think what he'll be like *now!*"

Tess shook her head. "It isn't right. No one has the right to push other kids around."

"Hi, guys," called a voice over the fence.

"Hi, Mrs. P.," Roger said.

Mrs. Pilkington stood next to her clothesline. She scooped a bedsheet out of her laundry basket and fastened it to the line with plastic clothespins.

"How's your problem coming with that boy at school?" Mrs. Pilkington asked. "The bully?"

Roger sighed deeply. "That's just what we were talking about."

"Come on over," Mrs. P. called. "I want to hear the latest."

The kids trooped over to Mrs. P.'s yard.

"We've tried everything we can think of!" Tess said. "The bodyguard idea didn't work. Then Ben tried to scare him over the phone by pretending to be a ghost."

"Those are certainly imaginative ideas," Mrs. P. said.

"But they didn't work!" Ben said.

"Did you try asking God for help?" Mrs. P. asked.

"Yeah!" Tess said. "But He must have been busy or something, because He didn't help us at all!"

"Yeah," Ben said. "I asked Him to make

David Halstead really scary so Brad wouldn't dare beat us up again."

"Oh," said Mrs. P. "Well, I think I know what your problem might be."

"What?" Tess asked.

"You told God what you wanted Him to do," Mrs. Pilkington said. "But God wants you to tell Him your problem and then turn the whole thing over to Him. He'll do things His own way. You just need to let go of the problem long enough to let Him work things out."

"Really?" Roger said.

"Sure," Mrs. P. said. "Listen, I have an idea. Do you know that Jesus said we should pray for our enemies?" The kids nodded. "Well, why not pray for this boy?"

Ben's eyes got big. "Are you kidding! Pray for Brad Garth?"

Tess made a gagging noise. "Yuck! Why would we want to pray for that jerk?"

"Yeah!" chimed in Roger. "He's mean, and we hate him!"

"He's just the sort of person who needs your prayers," said Mrs. Pilkington. "And while you're at it, ask God to solve your problem for you. Then let the problem go and don't think about it anymore. When the thought of Brad Garth comes into your mind, ask God to bless him and then gently put another thought in Brad's place."

The kids looked at one another.

"I don't know," Tess said doubtfully. "I don't feel like asking God to bless that rat."

"Well," Mrs. P. said thoughtfully, "how about just trying it as an experiment?"

"An experiment?" Ben said.

"Sure," said Mrs. P. "Just try it and see what happens."

Ben looked at Tess, then Roger. He shrugged. "Well," he said, "we've tried everything else we can think of. Maybe we should give this a try."

"Okay," Roger said. "I'll do it."

Tess sighed. "Me too. But my mother says that God knows what's really in our hearts. Don't you think He'll know we really don't like Brad?"

"Oh, sure," Mrs. P. said. "But He'll also hear you asking for blessings for Brad. I think it will make God happy to know you're praying for someone even though you don't like him very much." Mrs. P. paused. "You know, it's easy to pray for your friends and family. Praying for enemies is a lot harder. God knows that too."

"I think maybe I can do it," Ben said.

"Sure you can," Mrs. P. said. "Just give God a chance to work things out. He's a lot smarter than we are! He'll do just the right thing. You wait and see."

"That sure would be great," Tess said.

"Yeah," Roger said. "I'm sick of thinking and worrying about Brad all the time."

"Good," said Mrs. P. "Because you don't have to worry anymore. Not when you remember that God is in control."

"I'm going home right now," Tess said. "I'll go to my room and talk to God for awhile."

"Good idea," said Mrs. P.

"Me too," said Roger and Ben.

Ben felt better. Maybe this was finally the answer: God is in charge.

We'll get out of the way and let Him do His work.

The Bully Gets Bullied

The Tree House Kids met the next morning on the sidewalk near the woods.

"Think we should take the shortcut?" Roger said.

"Did you pray for the Beast last night?" Tess asked.

"Yup," Roger said. "I asked God to bless him and solve our bully problem. How about you guys?"

"Me too," Ben said.

"So did I," Tess said. "But I told God it wasn't easy to ask for blessings for Brad."

"Yeah," Roger said. "Well, you think we should take a chance with the shortcut?"

"Yeah," Ben said. "Somehow, I feel a little better about Brad."

Tess's mouth dropped open in surprise. "You do?"

"Oh, I don't like him," Ben said, "and I still think he's a jerk. But after I asked God for help, I didn't feel so scared anymore. I don't know, I guess it was just good to know that God was going to help us."

"Yeah, I know what you mean," Roger said. "I felt the same way."

"Well, I'm still pretty scared," said Tess. "But if you guys want to go through the woods, I'll go with you."

"Okay," Roger said. "Let's go."

The three kids moved into the woods. Tess looked around cautiously every three or four steps, afraid to see Brad Garth.

"Both times we've seen him he was at the top of the slope," Tess said.

"Bless Brad Garth," Ben whispered.

"Bless Brad Garth," said Roger.

"Ditto," said Tess.

"That's no prayer," Ben said.

"Bless Brad Garth," said Tess.

The kids climbed to the top of the slope.

"He isn't here," said Roger. He looked at his watch. "I guess we're a little early."

"That's okay," said Tess. "Let's keep moving."

The kids walked the rest of the way to school without seeing Brad.

In fact, except for once when Brad quickly walked by Ben in the hall, the kids didn't see him at all during the school day. He didn't even appear on the sidewalk after school.

"Well, that's one whole day without getting bullied by Brad," Roger said on the way home.

"But we didn't even see him," Tess said. "So it really doesn't count."

"Let's not talk about it," Ben said. "We told God we'd let Him handle it, so let's just do what we'd do normally."

"Okay," Tess said. "Let's stop at the 7-Eleven, okay? I want some gum."

"Yeah," Roger said. "I've got an extra 50 cents. I emptied the wastebaskets and took the garbage out to the curb this morning."

"Okay," Ben said. "Let's go."

The 7-Eleven was only a couple of blocks out of the way. The kids arrived there less than 10 minutes later.

They pushed open the heavy glass doors and went inside.

Tess hurried over to the stand filled with gum and candy.

"Bubble gum's my favorite," she said. "Purple grape."

Just then Roger grabbed her hand and Ben's arm. His face went white, and he pointed silently to the glass door.

Brad Garth was coming through the door. He was with a big man with dark hair.

The three kids quietly drew back behind one of the shelves. They were just tall enough to see Brad over the shelf without drawing his attention.

The man walked to the back of the store and yanked open the door to the refrigerator section that held soda and beer. Meanwhile, Brad walked slowly along the front, looking at the bags of chips and snacks displayed in the wire racks near the front door.

The man grabbed a case of beer, slammed the refrigerator door, and tromped back up the aisle. He didn't seem too steady on his feet, Ben thought.

"What are you doin'?" he growled at Brad. "Get over here."

Brad held up a bag of chips. "Can I get these chips, Dad?" he asked.

"No, and shut up about it," his dad said. "I only got enough money for the beer."

Brad made a face and angrily tossed the bag of chips back on the rack. He started walking to the cash register, but he caught his foot on the rack. Brad tripped and fell to the floor.

Brad's father turned around to see Brad sprawled on the floor. He swore loudly, threw some money on the counter to pay for the beer, then stalked over to his son.

He grabbed Brad's shirt behind the neck

and hauled the boy to his feet. "Clumsy kid," he said. "Come on, let's get out of here."

He roughly pushed Brad ahead of him out the door. The kids watched Brad and his father climb into an old car and drive away.

"Wow," Tess said softly. "Brad's father is mean."

"Yeah," Roger said. "Even meaner than Brad."

"I think Mr. Garth had been drinking," Ben said. "He looked kind of wobbly."

The kids paid for their gum and left the store.

"Gee, I kind of feel sorry for him," Ben said out on the sidewalk. "It'd be awful having a father like that."

"Yeah," Tess and Roger agreed.

"Well," Ben said. "At least now when we say prayers for Brad, we'll know what to ask for."

"What do you mean?" Tess said.

"Brad needs someone to like him!" Ben said.

"He sure does," Tess said, and Roger agreed.

God's Mysterious Ways

The next day before school, The Tree House Kids met at the edge of the woods.

"Did you bring it?" Tess said.

"Yup," said Roger. "That was a good idea you had, Ben."

Ben grinned. "I hope we see Brad Garth this morning."

"Can you believe that?" Tess said to Ben and Roger. "I never thought we'd *want* to see Brad Garth!"

"Me either," Roger said.

The three kids walked into the woods.

"I'm a little nervous," Tess said.

"Me too," Ben said. "But I think it'll be okay."

They walked into the deepest part of the woods and then up the slope.

And there he was.

Brad Garth was sitting on the tree stump. He stood up when he saw them coming and headed right toward them. He didn't slow down until he was right next to the kids, and then he stopped.

He gave Roger a little shove.

"Give me your lunch money," he said.

Roger looked up at Brad. He blinked behind his big glasses, but he didn't look scared at all.

"I don't have any lunch money with me, Brad," he said. "But I made an extra lunch for you."

Roger opened his book bag, stuck his hand in, and came up with a paper sack. He held it up to Brad.

"Want it?" he asked. "It's got some good stuff in it—a peanut butter and jelly sandwich, a banana, and a candy bar."

Brad stared at Roger. He didn't seem to know what to say.

"Go ahead," Roger said, still holding it out. "Take it."

Brad now eyed Roger with suspicion. "What'd you do, spit on it or something?"

Roger blinked again. "Heck, no. Why would I do that?"

"You want to eat lunch with us, Brad?" Tess asked.

"We eat at the table closest to the door going outside," Ben said. "That way we get to the playground sooner."

Brad stared at Ben, then at Tess, then at

Roger again. He still hadn't taken the lunch Roger had offered.

"You don't have to eat with us," Roger said. He shrugged. "It was just a suggestion."

Brad looked confused. He looked as if no one had ever been nice to him before.

He frowned. "I don't want to eat with you twerps," he said sourly.

"Okay," Roger said. "But here's a lunch for you anyway."

Brad scowled and yanked the lunch out of Roger's hand. He peeked inside.

"This better not have anything wrong with it," he said. "Or you'll be sorry."

"There's nothing wrong with it, Brad," Roger said in a matter-of-fact voice. "You'll like it. The peanut butter's the crunchy kind."

Brad continued to scowl. He looked at Roger. He looked at Ben. He looked at Tess.

Then, without another word, he turned and walked away.

The kids watched him go.

"Wow," Tess said softly. "Did you see how surprised he looked when Roger gave him the lunch?"

"I bet his dad doesn't give him lunch money," Ben said. "That's probably why he steals money from other kids."

"Yeah," Tess said. She looked at Roger. "You were great, Roger."

Roger grinned. "I wasn't even scared."

"Yeah," Ben said. "I wasn't, either. I guess when I saw his father acting mean to him—well, I started feeling sorry for him."

"Yeah," Tess said. "Me too."

"You know," Ben said. "I think our problem is getting solved. At least we're not afraid of Brad anymore."

"We know why he acts like a jerk," Roger said.

"Yeah," Tess said. "Maybe this praying stuff really does work. But God sure has a different way of fixing things."

"Yeah," Ben said. "I never thought we'd see Brad getting picked on! And I never thought we'd decide to be nice to him!"

"Well," Tess said, "you know what the Bible says about God."

"What?" Ben and Roger asked.

"God works in mysterious ways," Tess said.

"Boy," Ben said, "He sure does."

Fishers of Boys and Girls

"This is really awesome, Mrs. P.," Roger said, hooking a worm on his fishing hook. "Thanks for bringing us fishing with you."

"My pleasure," Mrs. Pilkington said. "This was my husband's favorite fishing place. He always said the fish like to gather here where the river bends."

"Did you fish with him a lot?" Tess asked.

"Yes," Mrs. P. said. "It gave us a chance to talk without the TV or the telephone interrupting us." She laughed. "Sometimes on our best fishing trips we didn't catch any fish, but we had some great conversations."

"Well," Ben said, "thanks again for the advice about Brad. We've seen him almost every day at school, and he hasn't been mean once!"

"Of course, we've fixed a lunch for him every day too," Tess said.

"Yes," Mrs. P. said. "That was a brilliant idea, Ben." Ben grinned. "But, you know," Mrs. P. said, "I think maybe Brad stopped being mean because you were nice to him."

"But I thought it was our prayers!" Tess said.

"Oh, that was a very important part of it," said Mrs. P. "But maybe God worked a little on you three kids, too, along with Brad."

"Us?" Ben asked.

"Sure," said Mrs. P. "I think when you ask for blessings for other people, God gives *you* blessings too. And maybe He opened your hearts to Brad. He knew it was hard for you to like the boy." She paused. "Be sure to thank God for helping you with Brad."

"Oh, yeah," said Tess. "I forgot."

"Do you think it was a coincidence that we saw Brad and his father at the 7-Eleven?" asked Roger.

"I don't know," said Mrs. P., "but I've learned that when I ask God to take care of my problems, all kinds of 'coincidences' happen. Seeing Brad with his dad helped to solve the problem."

"Yeah," said Ben.

"Oh, boy," Roger said, looking off in the distance. "Speaking of coincidences . . ." He nodded toward something over their shoulders.

"It's Brad!" Tess whispered to Mrs. P.

And there he was. Brad was standing in the distance among the trees.

Roger waved to him, and then Ben and Tess waved too.

Brad didn't wave back, but he approached slowly. When he was close, Ben said, "Hi, Brad."

Brad didn't answer.

"Want to fish with us?" asked Roger. Brad shrugged but didn't speak. "You can use my pole for awhile."

"That isn't necessary, Roger," said Mrs. P. "I have an extra pole. It belonged to my husband. Why don't you run and get it?" She handed Roger a key. "It's in the trunk with the rest of the fishing gear."

Roger took the key and scooted off.

Brad stood quietly. He still hadn't said anything.

"Come on and sit down," Tess said to Brad. "This is a great spot for fishing."

"Even though we haven't caught anything yet," said Ben.

"Even though we haven't even had a nibble yet," said Mrs. P., laughing.

Brad came over and sat on the bank of the river, but he still didn't speak. He kept his gaze fixed on the far side of the river.

Roger came back with the fishing pole from Mrs. Pilkington's car and handed it to Brad.

"Here are some worms," Ben said, passing an old margarine tub to Tess, who handed it to Brad.

Brad poked his finger in the dirt until he found a worm. He pulled it out and hooked it on his line. Then he dropped the line in the water.

"Beautiful day to fish," Mrs. P. said, staring off into the trees across the river.

"Yeah," Tess said.

The five of them sat quietly, gazing into the river.

"How do you like your fourth-grade teacher, Brad?" Tess asked. "Mrs. Street?"

Brad shrugged. "She's okay."

"She looks nice," Tess said.

All at once, the bobber on Brad's line began dancing wildly on the surface of the water. Then it ducked below the water and popped back up.

"You've got a fish!" cried Tess.

"All right!" yelled Ben.

"Bring it in nice and easy," said Roger. He set down his pole and hurried to Brad's side.

Brad's eyes grew big, and he sat forward, his mouth set in a tight, straight line. "Come on, come on," he whispered.

Brad reeled in his line slowly and pulled the fish out of the water.

"That's a beaut!" Ben said, looking at the fish flip-flopping on the end of Brad's line.

"Good work, Brad," Roger said, clapping Brad on the shoulder.

"You can have it for dinner," Mrs. P. said.

For the first time, the kids saw Brad smile. It wasn't a little smile or a mean smile.

No, this was a big, all-over-the-face grin that lit up his eyes and set a glow around him.

Ben watched Brad's face and felt very happy himself. He knew that Brad might not become one of his best friends. But this was a start. A small start, but certainly a step in the right direction.

Ben felt good about his new friend Roger, too, and their club, The Tree House Kids. Now that their problem with Brad was taken care of, they could just have fun together.

But best of all, Ben thought, now he and Tess and Roger knew how to solve problems. And it was so easy. Just hand them over to God and stand back. Good and surprising things were likely to happen.

And that was a very good feeling.